This book belongs to

miss sophy

GRIMM'S
FAIRY TALES

The Children's Classic Edition

GRIMM'S
FAIRY TALES

The Children's Classic Edition

RETOLD BY DAVID BORGENICHT

With illustrations by

ROBIN LAWRIE, GRAHAM PERCY,

JENNY WILLIAMS AND ROBERT WILSON

Colour
Library
Direct

CLD 20668
This edition published in 1998 for Colour Library Direct,
Godalming Business Centre, Woolsack Way,
Godalming, Surrey GU7 1XW
Printed in China

Cover and interior design by Ian Butterworth
Cover illustration by Robert Wilson
Interior illustrations by Robin Lawrie, Graham Percy, Jenny Williams, Robert Wilson
Edited by Mary McGuire
Set in Berkeley

Published by Courage Books, an imprint of
Running Press Book Publishers
125 South Twenty-second Street
Philadelphia, Pennsylvania 19103-4399

INTRODUCTION

Once upon a time, there were two brothers named Jacob and Wilhelm Grimm. They lived in Germany, in the early nineteenth century. The brothers were both quite learned scholars, but times were hard, and they were often in dire need of money. To help put food on their table, they undertook different publishing projects — writing histories of the German language, compiling dictionaries, and publishing collections of traditional oral folktales, for which they are best known.

The Grimms became fascinated with the traditional stories that had been told for centuries at dinner tables, family gatherings, and children's bedtimes, and they decided to gather them for study. Over many years, the brothers invited many storytellers into their home to tell their tales, and thus *The Fairy Tales of the Brothers Grimm* was born.

This beautifully illustrated edition contains seven of the most beloved of the brothers' collected tales — "The Frog Prince," "The Fisherman and his Wife," "The Musicians of Bremen," "The Brave Little Tailor," "The Golden Goose," "Rumpelstiltskin," and "Hansel and Gretel." All the stories have been retold for today's young readers, from early translations of the original collections. These classic tales have been told and retold for many hundreds of years, but their true natures remain intact here — they are stories of powerful magic and of gentle honesty, of cruel witches and handsome princes, of beautiful princesses and mischievous children. But above all, they are stories of true love, of friendship, and of the dream we all share to live happily ever after.

CONTENTS

THE FROG PRINCE

There once lived a king with a beautiful young daughter. On hot days, the princess would go to a nearby forest and sit at the edge of a well to cool off. On one such day, the princess sat quietly beside the well, tossing her favorite golden ball high up in the air, and then catching it each time in her tiny hands. But one time, the ball did not fall into her outstretched hands. It hit the ground, rolled to the edge of the well, and went over—SPLASH!—right into the water.

The princess looked down into the deep, dark well. Her favorite ball was lost forever. She began to cry.

"What is the matter, little princess?" said a soft voice behind her.

The princess turned around, rubbed her eyes, and looked down at the head of a frog that was sticking out of a nearby puddle.

"Oh, frog," she said, sniffing a little. "My golden ball has fallen into the well."

"Well, stop crying," croaked the frog. "I can get your ball back." The princess's beautiful face lit up. "But first you must promise that you'll reward me with a kiss," the frog said.

"Oh yes! Yes! I promise! Just bring me back my ball!" she agreed. *Ugly frog!* she thought to herself. *He shall never get a kiss from me!*

Satisfied with her promise, the frog hopped into the well. Within moments he surfaced, holding the ball in his mouth.

The princess was so overjoyed to have her golden ball back that she picked it up and skipped with joy all the way back to the castle, without even thanking the frog.

The very next day, as the princess sat at dinner with her father, she heard someone knocking at the door.

"Princess," a voice called. "Open the door!"

Curious, the princess got up, opened the door, and there, right on the front stoop, sat the frog.

"What is it, child?" asked the king.

"It's a disgusting frog!" said the princess.

"What does he want?" asked the king.

And his daughter told him the whole story. "I never thought I'd have to keep the promise," she explained. "After all, he's a *frog* — YECHHH!"

"You made a promise," said the king. "You must keep it."

"I have come for the kiss you promised me," said the frog. The princess shuddered at the thought and began to cry. But the king looked at her sternly, and she lifted the frog up to her face. And as she looked into his eyes, she saw something strange in them — something beautiful. Then she gave the frog a quick kiss and gently set him down on the floor.

Suddenly, the frog was transformed into a handsome prince — with kind and beautiful eyes!

"Thank goodness the spell is broken," said the prince, looking with amazement at his fingers and hands. "I was bewitched by an enchantress many years ago, and nothing but the tender kiss of the king's fair daughter — you— could save me. Thank you."

The princess was embarrassed by how she'd treated the frog prince. "I'm sorry I was so mean to you," said the princess. "Will you forgive me?"

"I will indeed," said the prince. "If you remember that all things are not as they seem — and if you promise to always keep your word."

The princess smiled brightly. "I promise," she said.

And they lived happily ever after.

RUMPELSTILTSKIN

There was once a very poor miller who had a beautiful daughter. She was the pride of his life. One day, the miller was ordered to appear before the king to offer a gift of honor to the royal family. But the miller had nothing to offer, so he went to the king's castle empty-handed.

"What gift have you brought?" asked the king gruffly.

The miller was so nervous that he spoke without thinking. "I — I have a daughter, who — who can spin straw into gold!"

The king was impressed but not convinced. "That's something I'd like to see," he said. "Bring her to the palace tomorrow."

The miller nodded and went home. He was so ashamed by what he'd told the king that he couldn't tell his daughter the truth. Instead, he told her that the king wished to meet her.

The next day, the king sent his coach for the miller's daughter. Once inside the castle, she was taken to a small room in a tall tower. The room was filled with piles and piles of straw! In the corner was a spinning wheel, a stool, and a reel.

The miller's daughter didn't know what to think, and as she stood looking at the spinning wheel, the king appeared at the doorway.

"Ah, mistress miller. Your father has told me that you can spin straw into gold," said the king. "You have one day to show me this trick. If you do not, your father shall die." With that, he turned and locked the door, leaving the miller's daughter alone.

Now, the miller's daughter had never even spun cloth, let alone straw into gold. She had no idea what to do and began to weep.

Then she heard a voice at the window. "My dear, why are you crying?" the voice asked.

The girl turned to see a strange little man. He looked to be very old, but he jumped and skipped around like a child.

"I have to spin all this straw into gold," the girl answered. "And I don't know how."

The little man smiled a crooked smile. "What will you offer me if I do it?" he asked.

"My necklace," said the girl, showing the man a beautiful silver locket that her mother had left her.

"Done," said the little man, hopping over to the wheel.

WHIR, WHIR, WHIR — in three turns, the reel was full of gold! He did this again and again, until morning came, and where the straw had once been were now stacks and stacks of pure, glittering gold.

When the little man was done, he grabbed the necklace, nodded to the miller's daughter, and jumped out the window. Just then, the king appeared at the doorway.

The king smiled greedily at the sight of his newly spun riches. But it wasn't enough. He had the guards bring the miller's daughter ten times more straw than before.

"Spin this straw into gold as well, and you shall become my queen," the king commanded. Then he locked the door once more.

The miller's daughter began to cry. Just as she was about to give up hope, she heard something behind her.

"What, more tears?" asked a familiar voice behind her. She turned, and saw the strange man again. "What will you give me if I help you this time?" he asked.

"I have nothing left to offer," the girl wept.

"Hmmmm," said the strange little man, rubbing his chin. "Then how about making a promise? When you become queen, you will give me your first-born child."

The miller's daughter thought to herself: *The king can't be serious about making me his queen. So I'll probably never have to give this strange man anything.*

"Agreed," said the girl finally. And so the little man began to spin again, faster than ever before. In the morning, once again, the room was filled with stacks of gold.

"Remember your promise," said the little man, nodding to the miller's daughter. Then he jumped out the window.

When the king came to the door and found the room filled with gold, he was overjoyed. And with the miller's happy consent, he married the girl that very day.

One year passed and the queen gave birth to a beautiful child whom she loved very much. As she was putting the baby to bed one night, she heard a strange but familiar voice. "I've come for what you promised me," the voice said.

She turned in horror, and saw the strange little man at the window, tapping his foot impatiently.

The queen wept. "I will give you all the riches of the kingdom if you want — just don't take my child."

The little man shook his head and smirked. "A promise is a promise."

But the queen begged the little man to give her another chance.

"All right," said the little man. "If in three days' time you discover my name, you may keep the child." And with that, he was gone.

The queen was grateful for the chance to keep her child, but she had no idea what the strange little man's name might be. She spent all of the next day thinking of the names she knew. That night, the little man appeared.

"Have you guessed my name?" he asked gleefully.

"Ferdinand?"

"No."

"Archibald?"

"No!"

"Mercutio?"

"No!" responded the little man, again, and again. And when morning came, the queen had not slept — and she had still not guessed his name.

"Only two days left!" said the little man with a giggle.

That day, she gathered even more names, and when the little man appeared that night again, she tried again.

"Is it Shishkabob? Or Ludwig? Or Twinkletoes?" asked the queen hopefully.

"No, no, and no!" said the little man, dancing. She guessed again and again, but his answer was always "No!" Finally, morning came, and he left.

On the final day, the queen sent messengers around the kingdom to discover names she had never heard of. And just when she thought there was no hope of keeping her baby, one of the messengers brought the queen some interesting news.

While he was out walking near a great forest, he

saw a little house with a fire burning in front of it. He walked closer, and hid behind a tree. A strange little man was hopping on one leg, singing this little song:

Nobody knows what I am called,

Nobody knows my fame!

Tomorrow I shall win my child

For Rumpelstiltskin is my name!

Well, you can imagine how happy the queen was to hear the messenger's report. She promised him a great reward, and waited until nightfall for the little man to appear.

"Last chance, your highness," laughed the little man, popping in through the window. "What's my name?"

"Hmmmm. Is it Harry?" said the queen slyly.

"No!"

"Gunther?"

"No!"

"Well," said the queen, finally. "Then it must be *Rumpelstiltskin!*"

"What! How did you know? Who has played a trick on me?" The strange little man began to yell, and stomp his feet, and shake his fists. In fact, he jumped up and down so hard that he plunged deep into the earth.

And he never came back again.

THE FISHERMAN AND HIS WIFE

There was once a poor fisherman and his wife who lived in a shack near the sea. Every day the fisherman took his boat out in the water and fished, until the sun began to set. He then went home to his wife, who cooked his daily catch. They were happy with their lives.

One day, as the fisherman sat in his boat, staring into the water, he felt a great tug at his line. His reel spun fast, and the line dived deep into the sea. With all his might and speed the fisherman reeled the line in and found a huge fish at the end of it.

The fish twitched in the air, and then — spoke. "Please, kind fisherman, let me live. I am not really a live fish after all — I am a prince, enchanted by a wicked spell. I would not taste very good anyway, so please let me go."

Well, the fisherman was not interested in eating a talking fish. So he bowed to the fish, wished him well, and set him free.

It was getting late, so the fisherman pulled in his line and rowed for home.

"Did you not catch anything today?" said the wife, who met him at the door.

"Not really," said the fisherman, mumbling. "I caught a fish, but he said he was really an enchanted prince, so I threw him back."

"And you didn't even ask him to grant you a wish first?" asked his wife in disbelief.

"What would I have wished for?"

"Well," said the wife. "You might have asked for a nicer house. You must go back and ask him to grant you this wish."

The fisherman knew that to argue with his wife was pointless. So he put on his fishing hat and went back out to sea.

He rowed out to the same spot where he saw the fish earlier, and called out at the top of his voice. "Enchanted prince! It is I, the fisherman who spared your life. Come to the surface!"

Suddenly, he heard a SPLASH! behind him, and up came the fish.

"What is it?" asked the fish.

"It is my wife. She wants you to grant us a wish for my having saved your life."

"What does she want?"

"She wants a nicer house to live in," explained the fisherman.

"Go home to your nice house," said the magical fish. And with a jump, the fish swam away.

When the man returned home, sure enough, he found a nice little house, with a nice little bench in front of it. His wife was sitting on the bench, smiling.

"Now isn't this better?" she said when the fisherman walked up. "Why, we can live here quite happily for many years to come!"

And they were very happy, too — for about a week. As the fisherman came in from his boat one night, his wife stood at the front door, tapping her foot impatiently.

"This house is too small for us," she said. "That silly fish could have given us a much bigger house. I think I'd like a stone castle better — go ask him for one!"

The fisherman was speechless. "This house is much better than the shack we had before," he said finally. "Why do we need a castle?"

"Just go and ask," said the wife.

And so, the fisherman went back to his boat, and rowed out to the spot where he had met the fish. The sky was gray, and the sea, which had been calm and deep blue earlier, was now rough and dark blue.

Again he called to the fish, and again it came.

"What does she want now?" asked the fish.

"She wants a castle," said the fisherman.

The fish waved his fin in the air.

"Go then," said the fish. "She is waiting for you by the drawbridge." And with that, the fish disappeared into the stirring seas.

The man rowed back to where the house had been, and there, in its place, was a great stone castle, just as the fish had told him.

His wife was waiting to show him the palace, which was paved with marble and decorated with gold.

"Isn't it wonderful?" she asked him.

"It is indeed," said the fisherman. "Now let's enjoy our new lives in our wonderful castle." And so they did — until the next week. The fisherman had just woken up, when his wife walked in.

"Get up! Get up! Look out the window," the wife said. "Look at all the land out there. It could be ours — if we asked for it. Go and ask the fish this instant to make me the ruler of all the land. I will not be happy unless you do."

The fisherman rubbed his eyes and shook his head. He knew that he would go back to the magical fish, but he knew it was wrong.

That day, when he reached the spot again, the sea was a deep gray. The waves rose up high over the sides of the boat, and the fisherman had to struggle to keep it from tipping over.

He called the fish again, and the fish came up.

"What does she want now?" asked the magical fish.

"She wants to be the ruler of all the land," the fisherman said, ashamed.

"Go back, then," said the fish, irritated. "You have what you came for."

The fisherman returned, and when he got to the castle, he saw that it was much larger,

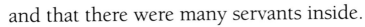

and that there were many servants inside.

His wife was sitting on a throne in her chambers when the fisherman entered.

"Are you happy now, my wife?" asked the fisherman.

"I am indeed, my dear," she said.

And so she was — for another week.

"Husband," said his wife one night, over their royal dinner. "I am unhappy. Being ruler of all the land is one thing, but there must surely be more to life than this. Only God knows for sure — so I would like to be just like God. Go now, and ask the fish to make it so."

"I will not," said the fisherman. "The fish has given us all we asked for. We deserve no more."

But the wife would hear none of it. "I want to be just like God," she said. "Go ask the fish for it now!"

And so he did. The sea was as black as midnight, and the waves were mighty. He called out to the fish again, the crashing of the waves almost drowning out his words.

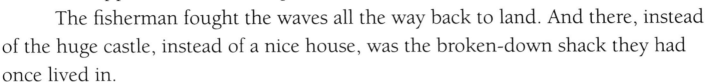

The fish swam to the surface. "What more could she possibly want?" asked the fish.

"She wishes to be just like God," said the fisherman, embarrassed to even speak the words.

"Go home," said the magical fish, waving his fin in the air. "She is just like God. And never again come out to speak with me." With a swish of his tail, the fish disappeared into the deep black sea.

The fisherman fought the waves all the way back to land. And there, instead of the huge castle, instead of a nice house, was the broken-down shack they had once lived in.

His wife stood in front, dressed in the same old clothes that she used to wear.

And the sea had returned to a placid blue. Life was back to normal. For just as the fish promised, the fisherman and his wife were indeed like God — as we all are.

Hans

Sarah
15

HANSEL AND GRETEL

At the edge of a great, dark forest, there once lived a young boy and girl named Hansel and Gretel. They lived in a small hut with their father, a woodcutter, and their mean stepmother, who didn't much like the children. A famine had fallen upon the land, and there was very little to eat. The woodcutter's wife blamed the children for their difficulties.

There would be plenty of food for us, the selfish woman thought, *if only these children weren't here.* And so, she hatched an evil plan to get rid of poor Hansel and Gretel.

One night, after the children had gone to sleep, the woodcutter groaned to his wife, "There isn't enough food in the land for us, my love. How will we feed our children, let alone ourselves?"

"Fear not, my dear," she said. "I have a solution. I will take them into the forest where fruits and berries are plentiful, and leave them there to live. Then we will have enough food to eat. It is the only way for all of us to survive."

"I hope you're not mistaken," said the woodcutter sadly.

His wife smiled. "Don't worry, my love. I know exactly what I'm doing."

And with that, they went to sleep. What the wife didn't know was that the children had heard the entire conversation.

"Gretel, what shall we do?" cried Hansel.

"If only we knew the forest better, we could sneak back to the house after our stepmother leaves — but we have no way to find our way home!" Gretel said.

The next day, after their chores were done, Hansel and Gretel's stepmother announced that it was time for them gather berries in the forest together. She gave them both a piece of dry bread for their suppers, and led them on their way.

Hansel realized he could use the bread crumbs to mark the trail back home!

In his pocket he broke the bread into small pieces, and threw them out onto the path as they walked on, deeper and deeper into the forest.

After they gathered the berries the children were quite tired. Their stepmother told them to rest while she finished the job. But as soon as they were asleep she ran back home, leaving them in the deep, dark forest.

Hansel and Gretel awoke to the strange night sounds, and saw the moon glowing brightly above them.

"Come!" said Hansel. "Let's find the crumbs and trace the path home!" And they got up to find the crumbs they had left behind.

But they found nothing. The crumbs had been eaten by birds and squirrels. They had no way to get home!

Hansel and Gretel walked the whole night, searching for the path. But every way looked the same. Finally they huddled together by the trunk of a great tree, wondering what would become of them.

The next morning, they were awakened by the song of a bird, which led them to the most amazing house they'd ever seen.

It was a tiny little cottage — built of gingerbread and icing. Its roof was made of cake and gumdrops, and its windows were made of pure sugar!

"Hansel, look!" said Gretel. "Food!" And immediately she broke off a piece of the roof and began to eat.

Hansel was excited, too, and he bit off a piece of the window.

Suddenly, they heard a voice inside the house:

> *"Nibble, nibble, like a mouse*
> *Who is nibbling at my house?"*

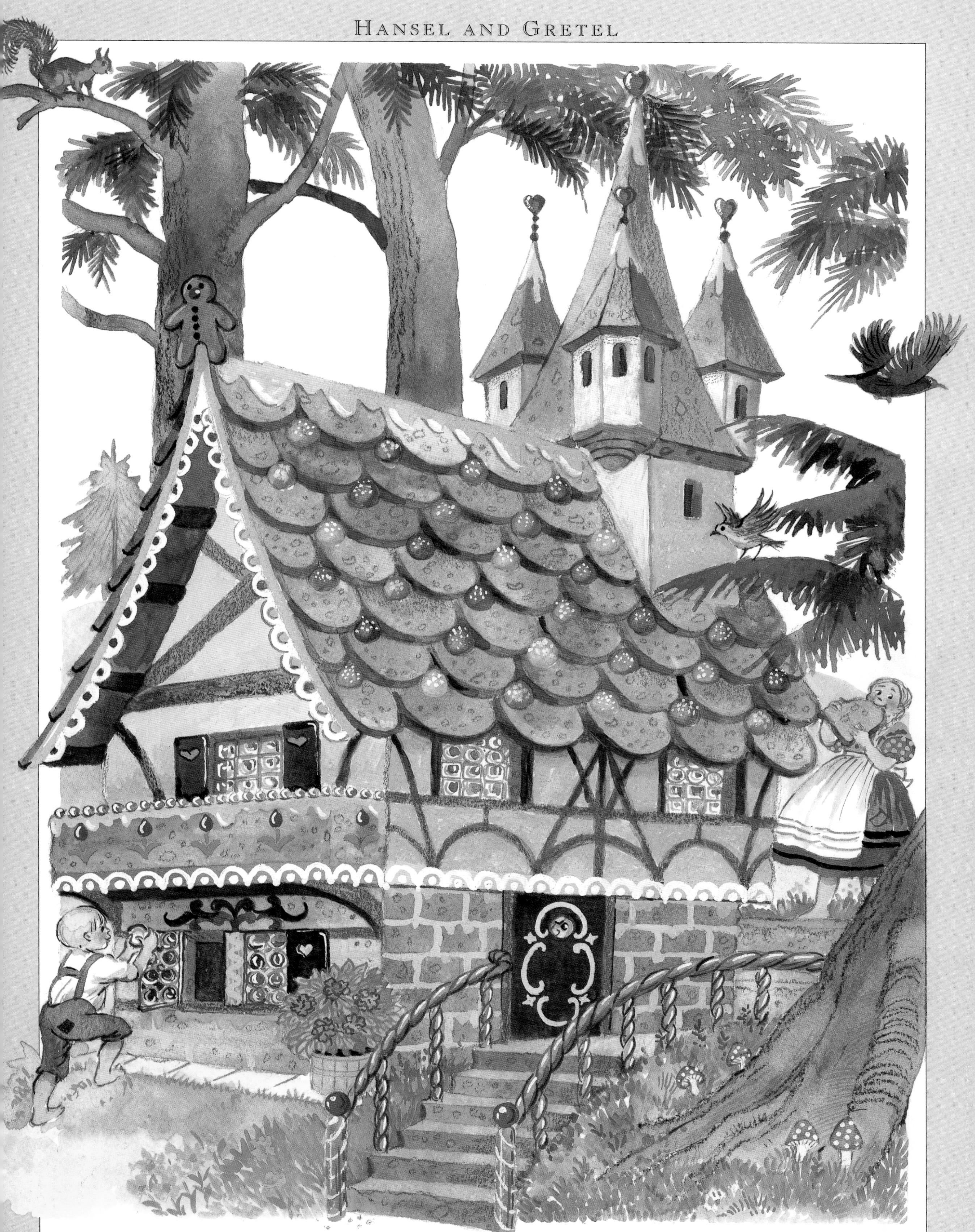

The children giggled with their mouths full, and they answered quickly:

"We cannot lie: we speak the truth
The wind is nibbling at your roof."

And then they laughed and went on eating — until the door of the cottage flew open, and out came an ugly old woman.

"My dear children," the woman croaked, "why have you come to eat my home?"

"We were left by our stepmother to die in the forest," said Gretel. "Please forgive us for eating your cottage. But we're so hungry."

The old woman smiled a toothless grin. "Well, why don't you come inside to eat?" she asked.

She took them inside and fed them milk and pancakes. And then when they were finished, she tucked the children into bed.

As the old woman watched them sleep, her gentle smile changed into an evil frown. For the old woman who lived in the gingerbread house was really a wicked witch who ate lost children!

She looked at the two of them sleeping with their rosy cheeks and thought of what a good meal they would make. *I'll eat the boy first,* the witch thought. *The girl will take a lot more doing.*

As soon as the children were asleep, she scooped up Hansel and put him in a small, locked cage she kept hidden. Hansel screamed for Gretel to help him, but by the time she woke up, it was too late — Hansel was behind bars.

"Get up, lazybones!" said the witch to Gretel. "I'm going to feast on your brother here, but first, we need to fatten him up a bit. Now go cook him something to eat."

Gretel knew there was nothing she could do as long as Hansel was imprisoned. She spent the day cooking and feeding Hansel, just as the witch instructed, fattening him up.

From time to time the witch checked on Hansel to see if he had gained any more weight. "Stick out your finger," she told him. But instead of a finger, he stuck out a small twig he had found in the cage.

"Aaaccch! Never any fatter," the witch said. "Gretel! get him some more food! He's still too thin to eat!"

After many days of feeding, the witch gave up.

"His weight is still the same!" the witch exclaimed. "I can't wait any longer." She turned to Gretel. "It's time to cook your brother. Now go and see if the oven is hot enough."

Gretel had to think quickly. She looked at the large oven the witch was pointing to, and she realized what the witch was trying to do — as soon as Gretel climbed inside the oven to check the heat, the witch would slam the door shut.

But Gretel wasn't going to fall for it.

"I don't know how," said Gretel to the witch.

"What do you mean you don't know how?" asked the witch. "Just crawl into the oven and see if the fire is hot enough."

" I don't think it's big enough," said Gretel.

"Stupid girl," the witch said, taking off her apron. "I'll show you what you do. Even *I* can fit in there." And she waddled up to the oven, opened the door, and stuck her head inside.

At that moment, Gretel ran behind the witch and gave her a big shove. She slammed the oven door and slipped a wooden spoon through the handles to lock it.

"Let me out! Let me out!" the witch cried. "I promise to never eat children again!"

But Gretel ran straight to the cage and let her brother out.

Hansel and Gretel and were so happy to be rid of the witch. They ran outside but didn't know which way to go.

Suddenly, they heard a bird sing. The bird that had led them to the house was sitting on a branch when they got outside.

"Hansel, look!" said Gretel, pointing to the bird.

Then the bird spoke. "You have released me from the witch's spell. Now I can once again fly free. How can I repay you?"

"You can take us home," said Gretel.

"Follow me," said the bird. In no time at all, they were home at their cottage.

Their father was out back, chopping wood.

"Father!" the children cried.

"Hansel! Gretel! Oh, I'm so happy to see you! " And he took his children in his arms and hugged them tightly. He told them of how he had not slept a moment since they had left, and of how their stepmother had died during the time they were lost in the forest.

"But as long as I have my Hansel and my Gretel back, life is good again," said their father. And they all lived together happily ever after.

The Musicians of Bremen

There once lived a donkey who had worked for his entire life for the same master. But one day, his master realized that the donkey was growing older and slower. It was time, the master told his wife, to send the donkey away. The donkey overheard his master's plan and decided to leave while he still could.

So that very night, the donkey chewed through his ropes, and set off on the road toward the town of Bremen. As he clip-clopped along the road, he hummed a little tune to himself, and he found that he quite enjoyed it. The donkey had always fancied himself as a musician. *Once in Bremen,* the donkey thought to himself, *I can surely be the town musician. After all, what other donkey sings as well as I do?*

A little ways down the road, the donkey came up to an old hound, who was lying down and gasping for breath.

"Why are you breathing so hard, old hound?" the donkey said.

"I have to run away from my master," the dog panted. "He thinks I am too old to hunt, and he wanted to have me put to sleep. So I ran away — but I don't know how I'll live."

The donkey smiled. "Come with me to Bremen, friend. I am going there to be the town musician, and perhaps you can join me."

"I can howl quite nicely," the hound said.

"Good," said the donkey. "Then come with me, and we will show them how music is played in Bremen."

And so off they went. Soon they came upon a cat lying on its belly in the road. Its face looked sad.

"Why the long face?" said the hound.

"How can I smile with my neck on the line?" the cat asked glumly. "I am old. I can no longer catch any mice — they just dance in front of me and taunt me all day. My mistress won't stand for it. She wants to do away with me, so I ran away. Now I don't know where to go."

"Come with us to Bremen," said the hound. "We're going there to be the town musicians."

"I do meow quite well," the cat said. "It's a deal; I'll join you!" And the cat got up, and joined them on the road to Bremen.

Not long after that, they came to a farm. It was the dead of night, and yet there, atop a fence post, sat an old rooster, crowing with all his might.

"Why do you crow when it's well before dawn, old rooster?" the hound asked.

"Because each crow may be my last," the rooster replied. "I am old, and I can't forecast the weather like I used to. My master told me that I will be tomorrow's meal. So I am crowing as loudly as I can — while I still can."

"Don't be silly," the donkey said. "Come with us to Bremen. We're going to become the town musicians, and we could surely use a voice as strong as yours."

The rooster didn't have much to lose, so he decided to join them. And so, the four musicians set off again on the road toward Bremen.

When the group came to a forest, they decided to spend the night. They found a great oak tree to sleep under, and were just about to settle in for the night when they noticed a light coming from a house nearby.

The donkey thought to himself: *If there is a house, that means there is food. And we haven't eaten for two days. Perhaps we could find some scraps there.* He roused his fellow musicians, told them of his find, and off they went to the little house.

As they got closer, they could see that the house was very run down. There was quite a bit of noise coming from inside.

The donkey, who was tallest, crept up to the window and looked inside.

"What do you see?" asked the rooster.

"I see a great feast, and a group of men in masks sitting at the table and laughing. They must be robbers," said the donkey.

But instead of running away, the

group decided that they were too hungry to let this opportunity pass. So they made a plan.

The hound hopped on the donkey's back, the cat hopped on top of the dog's back, and the rooster flew up onto the cat's head.

And at the count of three, they burst into song. The donkey brayed, the hound howled, the cat mewed, and the rooster crowed.

Frightened by the noise, the robbers stopped eating and laughing. At that moment, the animals broke through the window, landing on the table, and putting out all the candles.

Thinking they'd encountered a ghost, the robbers ran off, screaming and yelling into the forest.

When the robbers were far away, the donkey started laughing. "It worked!" he said. "Now we have the food to ourselves! We all made wonderful music."

And everyone agreed.

After their meal, the four musicians went to sleep.

But not far away, in the middle of the forest, the robbers were beginning to get curious about what had frightened them. And so they decided that one of them would go back to check up on the house.

The animals were asleep when the robber came back, but it was so dark that he couldn't see them. He walked right into the front door of the house. The first thing he saw was the cat's eyes, glowing in the night— but the robber thought they were coals in the fireplace. So he took a match from his pocket, struck it, and went to light the coals.

The cat jumped into the robber's face, scratching and spitting.

The robber rushed toward the back door — and tripped right over the hound, who woke up and bit him in the leg. The robber ran straight across the yard — right into the donkey, who gave him a strong, hard kick with his back feet. And the rooster, who was perched in the rafters, awoke from all the noise and began to crow, "Cock-a-doodle-doo! Cock-a-doodle-doo!"

The robber ran back to the forest and told his friends what he had seen.

"There's a witch in the house who spat on me and scratched my face with her talons. By the door stood her evil assistant, who stabbed me in the leg with a long knife, and in the yard is her huge beast, who beat me with a club. And if that's not enough, on the roof is the judge who cried out, 'Bring me the scoundrel! Bring me the scoundrel!' We should never go back there again."

They never did. And the musicians of Bremen lived quite happily in that little house for the rest of their days.

THE BRAVE LITTLE TAILOR

One day, a little tailor was making himself some breakfast when a swarm of flies gathered around his meal. "Who invited you?" the tailor asked the flies. The flies didn't answer. Annoyed, the little tailor grabbed a piece of cloth, and swatted at the flies. He killed a dozen of them with one blow.

The little tailor was quite proud of himself. *A dozen flies with one swat,* he thought. *Why, the whole kingdom should know about my bravery!* He made himself a new belt that very moment, on which he stitched the words "A dozen in one blow!"

And then, the little tailor, having decided that he was much too brave to be a mere tailor any longer, went off to seek his fortune.

He walked nearly twenty miles that day, and fell asleep by the side of the road. The next morning, before the tailor was awake, two royal guards from a nearby kingdom passed him on the way home.

They read the tailor's belt — A DOZEN IN ONE BLOW! — and were overjoyed. Their kingdom, you see, had been tortured for many years by two giants who lived nearby. The guards thought that the tailor's belt meant that he had killed a dozen men in one blow — they didn't know the belt referred to tiny flies. So they thought that the tailor was the one who could help them.

They shook him awake.

"Why do you awaken me?" asked the tailor.

"You must be a very brave man," said one of the guards. "And we are very much in need of a brave man." He explained about the giants that had been plaguing their kingdom, and told the tailor that the king had offered a vast reward to whoever could defeat the giants.

The tailor, still feeling quite proud, decided to join the guards, and together they made their way back to the castle.

"Well, you don't look like much to me," said the king. "But I wish you luck."

With that, the little tailor bowed, and went on his way, taking with him only a pouch of rocks as his weapon.

The forest was dark and gloomy, but the tailor didn't mind. He was happy

just thinking about how much his life had changed. Two days ago he was busy mending people's shirts and socks, and today he was the king's special warrior, off to rid the land of two horrible giants. He smiled at the thought.

Until he came upon the giants. They were sleeping under a tree. They were vicious-looking. They had hair all over their bodies, sharp, crooked teeth jutting out from their mouths, and snores that shook the trees above them. They were almost as loud as they were ugly.

The tailor decided to climb up the tree under which the giants were sleeping, in order to get a better view of the situation.

The tailor hid himself in the leaves so that no one could see him from below. He was busy deciding what to do next, when all of a sudden he slipped, his pouch fell open, and several stones tumbled out, hitting one of the giants on the forehead several times, and filling the other giant's ear with rocks. The giants woke up and looked around, seeing no one but each other to blame.

"What's the big idea?" said the giant with the dented forehead. "Why are you throwing rocks at me?"

"I think you're the one who's hurling rocks!" said the giant with the earful of stones.

"I am not," said the first giant, and turned his back on the other giant to look for someone else who might have thrown the stones. The other giant turned his back to look as well.

The tailor wasted no time at all. Quickly he took a few of the remaining rocks, and threw them as hard as he could at the two giants' heads. The rocks hit both of them at the same time, and stung them like a dozen bees.

"OUCH!" said the first giant.

"That SMARTS!" said the second. "And it's too bad for you that it does!" He rushed at the other giant, shoving him hard against the tree. The tree wavered back and forth, and the tailor almost lost his grip again.

The first giant got up, brushed himself off, and shoved the other giant as hard as he could into a large boulder, shattering it into a thousand pieces.

The fight got worse from there — until the two giants had finally beaten each other to death!

The tailor, who had been watching the whole episode safely up in his tree, climbed down once the ruckus was over. He smiled at his accidental cleverness, cut off the giants' heads as proof that they were dead, and returned to the king's castle.

"The giants are dead, your highness," said the tailor to the king. "Here's the proof," said the tailor. And with that, he opened the sack, and out tumbled the giants' heads.

The king, for the first time in many years, smiled. "You are a true warrior," he said to the tailor. "Was it difficult?"

"Truth be told," said the tailor, "I've had a harder time killing flies."

And so he had. The tailor received his reward, and went off again to help the world as best he could — as long as it didn't involve mending shirts and socks.

The Golden Goose

Once upon a time there lived a family with three sons. The youngest of these sons was called Simpleton, and his brothers teased him whenever they had the chance.

One day, the boys' parents sent them into the forest to cut some firewood — winter would be coming soon, and they needed to stock up. Their mother packed them each a lunch, but she only had enough cake and wine for two of the boys, so Simpleton was given crumbs and sour beer.

Not long after the boys entered the forest, they saw an old man walking up the path toward them. The man looked tired and hungry.

"Good day, young men," the old man creaked. "Please, I have not eaten for many days — do you have any food you can spare?"

The oldest son laughed at the old man. "Away, beggar," he said. "I have only enough wine and cake for myself." And he waved the old man away.

The second son responded selfishly too. "If I give you my food there will be none for me, old man," he said. "Now be off!"

But Simpleton felt sorry for the old man, and said, "I have only cake crumbs and sour beer, but I'd be happy to share it with you."

The old man's face lit up, and they sat down together on a nearby rock to eat their meal, as the brothers laughed at them and went off to chop wood. Amazingly, when Simpleton removed the sack of crumbs from his bag, he found that it had become a whole cake, and the sour beer had turned into the finest wine! He and the old man ate and drank well, and had quite a nice time.

"You have a good heart, boy," said the old man. "And because you've been so generous, I will give you a gift. It's in that tree over there." Simpleton looked at the tree the man was pointing to. But when he looked back, the old man was gone.

Meanwhile, just as the oldest son was about to cut into a tree he'd found, a mysterious force came over his ax and instead of hitting the tree, it cut the oldest son in the arm! And when the second son raised his ax to cut into the tree, a strange force also caused his ax to miss and cut into the boy's leg instead. The two boys limped all the way home.

But when Simpleton raised his ax to cut down the tree the old man had pointed to, he had no problem. In fact, as soon as he hit the tree, it fell over with a CRASH! And inside it, he found a golden goose. "Take me to the king," said the goose. "He will gladly pay you for such a rare treasure as me."

So Simpleton walked toward the kingdom. But it was getting late, so he stopped for the night at a nearby inn.

The innkeeper had three daughters who lived there, and when they saw Simpleton walking in with the strange and wonderful bird, they were entranced.

"I must know if the feathers are really made of gold," said the oldest daughter to her sisters.

So when Simpleton had fallen asleep, the oldest sister crept over to the goose and reached out to pluck out a feather. But as soon as she touched the goose, her hand became stuck! She pulled and pulled, but she could not get loose!

Minutes later, when their sister had still not emerged from the room, the other two crept into Simpleton's room to see what was wrong. When they saw their older sister, stuck fast to the goose, they tried to pull her free. But they too became stuck!

When Simpleton awoke the next morning, he saw the three sisters, all of them stuck to the goose, smiling sheepishly at him.

"It's about time you woke up," said the oldest sister rudely. "Now help us get free."

"I wish I could," said Simpleton. "But I don't know how. Besides, I have an appointment with the king." And with that, he picked up the goose, with the three girls still attached to it, and made his way down the road.

On the road they passed a farmer, who stared in disbelief at the pack of fools marching by. "Why don't you leave that boy alone?" he asked the sisters. And he grabbed the youngest sister's arm to pull her away. Now the farmer was stuck as well!

At the gates of the city, two guards stopped the group.

"Where do you think you're going?" one guard asked.

"I have something for the king," Simpleton explained.

"Then only you can go in," said the other guard, reaching for the farmer to pull him off.

"No, don't touch him!" shouted Simpleton. But it was too late. Now the guard, too, was stuck. Then the first guard grabbed for his partner, who also became stuck.

Simpleton pushed open the city gates and led the pack inside. Posted on the door inside was a royal decree, from the king himself. It said that his daughter had been sad for more than fifteen years, and that a great reward would come to whoever could make her laugh. Many had tried it before, but all had failed, the decree said. Simpleton decided to give it his best. He headed with the goose — and the sisters, and the farmer, and the guards — for the castle, and insisted on being taken to the king's daughter.

The group was led to a little room in a tower, and Simpleton peeked around the door. There, on a

throne, sat a beautiful but sad princess.

Simpleton waved, and made a face. The princess looked straight at him, but never even cracked a smile. Then he stepped inside, and brought the goose's head around the corner. This time, the princess's eyes lit up a bit, but quickly faded back to sadness.

Finally, Simpleton ran into the room holding the goose under his arm. Of course, following close behind were the three sisters, the farmer, and the guards — all flailing wildly. First the princess smiled, then grinned, then she burst into laughter.

She laughed so joyously that it broke the goose's spell and all the hangers-on — the sisters, the farmer, the guards — came free and fell flat on their backs. The princess laughed even harder, and then Simpleton joined in. Soon, everyone in the room — and then in the castle — was laughing!

"Who are you?" the king asked Simpleton, when the laughter had subsided.

"My name is Simpleton, and I am just a simple boy," he explained. "Someone who likes to help others."

"You have cheered up my daughter," said the king. "You may stay here and keep my daughter happy from now on."

"I will gladly contribute to your daughter's joy," said Simpleton.

And they all really did live happily in the kingdom for ever more.